D0315830

This Orchard
book belongs to

_____

_____

For Mrs Crawford,
with love and thanks for
all your encouragement.

ORCHARD BOOKS
338 Euston Road, London NW1 3BH
Orchard Books Australia
Level 17/207 Kent Street, Sydney, NSW 2000

First published in 2008 by Orchard Books
First paperback publication in 2009

ISBN 978 1 84616 942 7

Text and illustrations © Sam Lloyd 2008

The right of Sam Lloyd to be identified as the author and
illustrator of this work has been asserted by her in accordance
with the Copyright, Designs and Patents Act, 1988.

A CIP catalogue record for this book is available from the British Library.

1 3 5 7 9 10 8 6 4 2

Printed in Singapore

Orchard Books is a division of Hachette Children's Books, an Hachette Livre UK company.

Blazes
Fire Station

Chief Rhino
TO THE RESCUE

Sam Lloyd

ORCHARD BOOKS

Meet Fire Chief Rhino. He's one of the bravest animals in Whoops-a-Daisy World. Whenever there's a fire, you can always count on him to save the day.

Let's go inside Blazes Fire Station and look around.

Chief Rhino likes to stay in peak physical condition. You have to be strong to fight fires, although there hasn't been a big fire in Whoops-a-Daisy World for a long time . . .

. . . but suddenly Chief Rhino spots something!

"What the blazes?!" Chief Rhino exclaims.
"It looks like there's a fire at Number One,
House Row! It's time for me to save the day!"

Chief Rhino dashes into the recreation room.
"Attention team! Stop what you're doing.
We're needed, so let's go!"

"... and AWAY!"
Nee-nar, nee-nar roars the siren as they dash through Whoops-a-Daisy World.

Inside the fire engine, Chief Rhino briefs his team. "This fire is a whopper," he announces. "I need you all to be brave."

"Great balls of fire!" exclaims Chief Rhino. "This is even more serious than I thought! I'll need the ladder, the hose and the breathing apparatus. Moose, when I shout 'NOW' turn on the water!"

"Yes, Chief!" nods Moose.

"Stand back!" instructs Chief Rhino. "I'm going in!"

"Three . . . two . . . one . . . NOW, Moose! NOW!"

Whoosh!
Hooray! The water puts out the fire!

But, uh-oh . . . it was only
the flames of the hundred candles on
Great Granny Wrinkle's birthday cake!

"Flaming flumps of fire!" gasps Chief Rhino.
"How could I have made such a silly mistake?
Instead of saving the day, I've ruined it!"

"Now, don't you fret," smiles Great Granny Wrinkle.
"We all make mistakes. What's important is that
you were trying to help."
"But I've ruined your cake," sighs Chief Rhino.
"Not at all!" she giggles. "Elephants of my age
don't have many teeth left,
so mushy cake is perfect!"

That cheers up Chief Rhino, so, in his most
serious voice, he gives a very important command
to all the animals of Whoops-a-Daisy World.

"Let's give Great Granny Wrinkle
the most super-sizzling party ever!"
And they do . . .

. . . even with the soggy cake!